Life Poems by
Stefan A. Nicholson

Shadows
Anxiety &
Narrative

Hobart Tasmania
2019

Shadows, Anxiety and Narrative

Other books by:

Stefan Andrew Nicholson

'SAN Language Book of Instruction'

'Business Analysis Package'

'Peripheral Lives'

'Blind Familiarity'

'Symbolic Art Notation'

'JEMMA short stories'

'CIRCLE in a SPIRAL'

"SPY within a RUBY"

"DIAMOND for a RUBY"

"RUBY's COVERT MISSION" – coming mid 2019

And an original music CD – **'Pictures of Life'**

"Life is not a rigid road to follow dutifully at the whim of others who seek to control the wild spirit within you. Be aware of their dull limitations on how people should live. Unaware, they are the slaves to fashionable normality . . . indifferent towards self-improvement and self-awareness. You must rise above their failings to see the person you really are, then protect that realisation within your mind."

- Stefan Nicholson

Shadows, Anxiety and Narrative

First Edition 2019   printed-book

Copyright © 2019 Stefan Nicholson, Hobart Tasmania.

All rights reserved

Envirosupport Publishers

P.O. Box 370, South Hobart,

Tasmania, Australia 7004

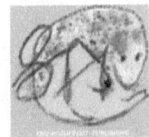

ISBN 978-0-6482953-8-9

978-0-6482953-8-9

Contacts:

Website: www.stefannicholson.com

Email: stefannicholson@bigpond.com
Phone: +61 417 181 077

BOOKS: https://www.amazon.com/author/stefannicholson

CONTENTS

INTRODUCTION

Writing . . . What on earth is that? I mean everyone writes. Everyone writes something. Don't they?

A creative writer writes what is on their mind, living through a story plot, talking about and sharing experiences with their characters in their mind (made up or real).

A poet can see and feel deeper things that are so real to their senses, but which may not be sensed by others until pointed out. Poetry also offers a unique way of writing which enhances the emotions conjured up by fleeting glimpses of imagery.

The ability to express yourself in writing after further thought and editing to strengthen your ideas is a mysterious thing, because the written word is permanent. It is then open to further interpretation by the reader . . . who may imagine the thoughts and ideas of the writer completely differently.

Living and dreaming are both real to the writer's mind, yet they reside in different dimensions of time and space, though we live only in the present, for the past has gone. The future is only a possibility based on how we live within each present moment and how we interact with random events that cross our chosen paths.

When I walk through the city or when I used to drive my maxi taxi to get myself away from my writing . . . sometimes waiting at a rank or outside a person's home or work . . . I see with a writer's mind:

I see the inner struggle of some aged, sick and homeless poor, betrayed to others by their looks, their actions and their faces.

I see from the innocent faces of children oblivious to most worldly problems, that they struggle between the importance of fighting for independence and belonging to a group.

I see the besotted looks on the faces of young lovers or the anger in the eyes of the wayward youth who is not understood and makes mistakes in desperation . . . if only for that one moment. Time that heals or time that is required to accept the help of others is often not at hand. We sometimes fail them.

I see the workers who march to work after surviving the gridlock to park their cars - oblivious to their surroundings and their peripheral vision – often glued to a digital device, yet juggling with the problems or excitement of their job or family at the back of their minds.

I also see much happiness, good fortune and caring in the world, which leads me to suggest that shadows, anxiety and depression are only temporary aberrations in our lives, providing there is someone to help us through the rough times and sad times. It used to be close family and not medication and restraint.

There has to be a balance of emotions to keep us from living too easily. Life is a challenge – look at what the other animals have to put up with in order to survive.

A good life was once living in a world of abundance and learning . . . learning to appreciate life for what it is . . . the life of your own making. But it may not be so for our children unless we act now to save what is left.

Our legacy should not be gloating documentaries of how much diversity of life there once was, before it was carelessly abandoned for our 'secluded' lifestyles.

"Out of sight, out of mind" . . . the motto of humankind.

Contrary to what the reader may think, the poems are not all about me. They are about my observations of the complex world that I see around me and those people who inhabit my conscience.

And finally, writing a typical love song is rarely a happy outcome – and once they are written, there is no love lost on their departure to a papery grave. It is much better to be in or out of love, rather than write about it.

Stefan Nicholson 2019 Hobart Tasmania

Together United

I watched with a sad heart the other day, wondering what I could do or say, to help you find your way.

To lift your spirits and share with you my take, on how to work with that what seems, if that what seems is fake.

For you know the seas will surely rise and wars will soon be fought, but there will never be an answer if you bury all these thoughts.

Yet by rising up together, you can demand a speedy change, from all those folks with power. Not one an honest sage.

There is always strength in numbers to show united might. Now wouldn't that in concert, be a shining light:

To sing together the anthem of refreshing youth.

To raise the stakes to seek exacting truth, even though they will fight to keep their greed, your hearts and minds will have set the seed.

For your time is here and now, and together we must rise, to demand they act to save this world. Rise up to fight their lies!

The Promise

I remember when I was four foot tall, with a cape and an umbrella but no planning for a fall.

Then I saw you staring from the shadows, out of the corner of my eye. That was the moment I fell in love. At the time, I knew not why.

We walked to school and shared our lunch, pretending not to care. Yet every day our feelings grew for we had formed a perfect pair, and you smiled one day, so fresh and sweet when I touched your ribboned hair.

Then you told me you were leaving, for your folks had broken up. As you cried, I softly held you, just like a little pup. It was then I knew I had changed forever, as I also felt your pain, so I made you pledge you would think of me, each time the full moon came.

How the years have passed so quickly as the moon did wax and wane. You will probably think I am silly, writing this. It seems totally insane, but I was told that you had kept our pledge – a promise to a little boy.

That you would think of him when the full moon came, to dream and share some joy.

Though I gaze into my cloudy mind, my eyes now no longer able, to see the moon which shines so bright, as round as my round table, I will ask the moon to say to you, that I have always thought of you the same. Yet at my window, I now pray for rest . . . and softly whisper out your name.

For I'm left with dreams, where the stars shine bright, and the full moon stares at that little boy, with a cape, an umbrella, standing four foot tall. I remember all the joy.

But the cold air seeks to draw me in. No more will I say again, the kindly words of our childhood pledge. . . for the full moon never came.

The Tallest Trees

Do you ever have that feeling? You know . . . on those days of just not knowing, what those in power are planning to do, on our downward slide to where life is going . . . inside a tunnel and down a hollow . . . convincing many of us to blindly follow.

And when all you want is peace and calm, amongst the tallest trees, high above the human plain, amid the screams of the forest's pain:

For these tallest links bind a delicate chain,

Broken by our acts insane,

Neglecting balance of loss with gain,

Thinking we were the kings of Earth's domain.

Now think of our children, imagining creatures from a picture book. As wide-eyed, they see how once they looked. Yet never chance to wondrous stare, at the beauty of nature's golden fare:

As the tallest trees gasp on putrid air,

As Earth succumbs, soon with no creatures there.

As their homeless future seems so bare.

As they die, with little food or drink to share.

Then they will know we did not care, for we robbed them by our stealth. Yet we will be gone. We will not be there, leaving a broken world from our squandered wealth, and a legacy of induced poor health.

But they will have learnt much from lessons past, that when greed and power rule to place others last, and when the seeds of destruction have been fully cast, then famine and war will rise up fast.

The Oyster

The Oyster is a harmless soul who lives beneath the changing tides.

Keeping to itself it takes no sides, feeding quietly where its secret hides.

But no longer, for we say that some are 'blessed', when a speck of grit fouls its silvery nest.

Our Earth is as the Oyster's life, for commercial gain has plundered its wealth, and we take it with greed, much more than we need, at the expense of its finite health.

And like the caged hen, whose last stolen egg ascertains it will soon be plucked, the oyster is attacked by a feverish hand as we comically say it is 'shucked'.

Yet, another word often springs to mind, which careless people use.

Sometimes to joke or curse, or randomly say . . . and sometimes to hurl abuse, but I will save it for our future world, which now shares a common fate.

For "The world is my oyster" they say . . . and we consume both at an extravagant rate.

Self Pity

I look to your eyes, but no longer feel at home.

The hurt reaches deep within me.

My sorry friend.

No one needs me now.

The music seems to cry, while the reality of life slips by,

And in my own life, sensitive to smiles and hidden annoyance,

Negative thoughts control my body.

Never – have I felt so lonely.

The Journey

I walk a path and continually find myself alone.

Nothing helps the emptiness and fears, of never finding home.

Not belonging to a place, or feeling part of the endless daydream we call time.

Like a paper boat swirling and dipping, through stormy seas unkind.

Looking straight ahead, daring new destinations to unwind

Against those my young life has traded new for old.

Hoping to find myself through peace of mind,

Which my daily dreams knowingly unfold.

Each facet of nature is so different giving experience of a kind

To help us journey onwards, for some place in our child's mind.

But I search with eyes so saddened when I dwell on what I've learned

For the journey is to nowhere, from where I never can return.

First Crush

Her name is known to me alone.

As I stare into daylight's play and night-time sleeplessness.

She has become my secret love.

A gentle thought of everything nice.

I care for her total state of being,

Her presence near and far, such radiant warm delight.

I can only watch from distant place,

Her soft, long flowing hair . . . angelic face.

She is like the whispers of sight and thought.

There is nothing else I would desire.

For without love, life's riches amount to nought.

I Saw Her Again

I saw her again, today!
Penetrating my world with a smile
To arrest my overwhelming curiosity
Which tease my thoughts of sensuous dare.
She seemed to focus my consuming interest
Giving promised hopes
With each and every secret stare

I felt her body's presence
More and more and more
As a passing slow but close caress
Left nature's musk perfume to test

As I gaze into her soft, misty eyes
And see her body so confidently poised,
Secrets flood across the ocean room.
She must know that I crave each moment
To lay by her receptive side

Her glances in quiet, pensive mood
Bathe me in warm reflections
Undying love it is said, will seek and find
It is true - as feelings rush my mind
This strange and timeless, close dream affair

Her presence makes me weak and faint
Intenseness now is hard to bear
She then pretends not to care!
Yet I feel her closeness ever more

While looking deep within her magic form

Wondrous images of strength and beauty combined

Marvelling at female presence – such strange ways

Our eyes linger a moment so brief

Yet sufficiently long as she feeds my senses

Awareness speaks from closed lips

In silent, knowing tongue

So softly she brushes against my back in passing

I feel her radiance

And savour moist sweet breath to my blushing cheek

Feelings remembered from romantic past

As she moves around with twisting form

Another touch is all I seek

And still, I stare at loose hair nestled

Around smooth, warm shoulders

I want to hold her close forever

I love that girl enough

Knowing that I should share emotions

Without second thought

Yes, I love her like I once but dreamed.

Feelings to always remember.

She must be told now before burning fire becomes smouldering embers.

I saw her again, today!

The Awakening

The day arrived when the awakening broke his fall. It was all there! Like a calling at silent dawn.

He choked, cried and finally sighed, at the new interpretation, of life's empty game. The solution was to hear the questions. The answers gave his mind the blame.

Why do we live by our fashions and fads? Trying on strange character roles, like actors on life's launching pads. Clinging to archaic ideas of a second eternal life, while the present one is wasted all trying to be the same. Always in conflict. Always in strife.

Make the most of how you can grow, and above all – be yourself, or you will look like everyone else, and your achievements will be 'off-the-shelf'. If you ignore these truths, and cling to other less demanding beliefs, then be damned in your supposed next life – with opportunities wasted, you are both victim and thief."

He studied the arts, science, philosophy and the past, living life to the full, adding another character to life's strange cast. So unique, with his caring and sharing, yet pausing to teach. Everyone gained from the former, and a few from his teaching, that he was able to reach.

The world saw his message in music and writings of truth as he helped the community with information, solutions to problems affecting the youth. And when the darkness was lifted, and ignorance removed, what was left was a calmness and minds that were soothed.

Already Taken

Look at his eyes and you know this man was her lover.

Hiding in the corner alone - with sad, dream-like gaze.

They all laugh at the wretch who now senses their sneers,

With emotional pain, for his conscience has ears.

Trying to search for reasons for his hopeless plight,

He dismisses even traces of truth. Foolish thoughts set in at night.

His sparkle, wit and love for life are drawing to a close.

He will never make his lover his wife – this he knows.

Her image and bouquet etched deeply on his tormented mind.

From that softness he remembers from a passionate bind,

Intimate touching and final binding caress.

Now see the pain on the face to his mind – his life is a mess!

Yes – the photograph I show to you is how it all began.

The searching for perfect love brought destruction for this man.

For love has taken its toll, until now (by his own hand), the loss of his life. The wife can become the lover, but rarely the lover the wife.

Take care my poor smitten friend, and learn this lesson true. Why only yesterday I took another photograph.

Look closely. Is that you?

Denying Self

I know a place where we belong – together.

It's in my dreams, and you know they last forever.

Forever and ever.

Please don't fade away. I want you to come and stay.

Not in my dreams – but in my life forever.

I'm part of your face, and I'm in your eyes reflection.

It's only the past that keeps me away, by your constant rejection.

Please don't turn away.

Why should I pay for others mistakes that I would never make?

Oh, never, never . . . never!

You talk of me as if I don't exist.

You are so clever . . . . so clever!

But I know your feelings for me match the list.

Although you say never. How simply clever.

Please let me see in your eyes, that the feelings you show are just lies.

Please.   Let me share in your life.

But this time forever . . . forever and ever.

Last Autumn Leaf

The sand of time is spilling from my heart,

And in my mind's confusion - sad eyes, hard life. Living only to exist.

Kindness returned by mistrust.

Lights shining through her hair.

"Can I take you for my wife?"

Red, flickering autumn lights, from soft, smooth shoulder-length hair.

Youthful beauty, girlish innocence – a woman on my mind.

"Soon"

Yet I saw behind tearful eyes, the unforgiving memories of childhood.

Those fatherless years

Conditioned for living, survival style - feeding off love and emotional fears

The deepest love - the woman she is to me.

She will leave me alone once more, all empty and bitter at the life that was given me for free,

Unable to love again, easy to hate - and at war with myself.

Secret Enigma

Something that has been shown throughout history,

are the shadows of dark minds within troubled souls

What magical brew can we drink to survive?

Innocent faces reach out with softness and feeling,

Without which I must be taken – through mystical ceiling.

One mind, one soul – as I search for the truth,

and the secrets of the cosmos.

Expression, ideas, creative thoughts from . . . without!

I must resist that which seeks me!

Is it that I am not intended to tell, that which I have found out?

Time and a Place

Now you're the biggest hypocrite around, for you look just like the others, and hide yourself with drugged ideas and alcoholic dreams.

All you have to do is find yourself, for you are only an individual mind who has lost sense of being and belonging, to the earth, from whence you came.

I'd like to help you out my friends. I've seen you – you must know me! I'm the end of life, which can never be turned around. Though no beginning, my freedom has many bounds.

Never colour the heavens at night! Armies of stars – those reds, those whites, surrounding weaker planets and shining bright, promising a better life, yet devouring by shadows – and starving all rights.

From where do we come, and how should we live? We are told how to think – and that we must constantly give.

But those to whom we give, they ask for our souls, so our stored life decays – just like the burning embers of coal.

Faded jeans and t-shirt club – what will you do when you grow old? No beliefs, no support, just outcasts who are united by hope. Your disgust with the world will force you to cope.

Though you may live as you like, and turn actor at will, the world remains greedily insane with environmental decline, increasing population, pollution and irrational hate.

You really deserve a better world . . . though I feel it is too late.

Hidden Truth

Religious sinners lurk, disguised in the park.

The minds of our children made blinder than dark.

Sad eyes grow from within their faces,

As they silently suffer from those who cover their traces.

Their fear struck first and logic was drowned.

Evasion of truths – yet the dulled crowd made no sound.

Others not there, with pain etched on their minds,

For they have traced throughout history, misuse by this kind.

Then business, media all lie to entice,

The striking for affluence. To wallow in vice.

Advertising pushing for greed in our culture,

Which to the youth in society is a soliciting vulture.

The pickings becoming new generation adults

The weakest inflicting the final insults,

Shadows of life, synthetic radicals – minds twisted and curled.

Dust and debris aren't the only things hurled,

As the flash in the sky blossoms upwards with reasons.

Your daughters bear sickness – the end of the seasons.

The seas strangely rise – and we climb to the sun!

Who or what was defeated, for if not you   . . . then who won?

The Musician

Well now at last it is time to die, though I have always laboured hard to try, even to find a single reason.

For as you I loved – I cannot lie. What a pathetic life, in such a joyous season.

My life you see was spoiled long ago, before I pained near death you know. And love . . . I could never find for long, by putting in an ordinary song – preserved my emotion. Yet even this was permanence only on manuscript.

When I was young and full of fun, my eyes of truth, they saw the sun.

It burned my mind so gradually that my age was known to me alone. All vision blurred. My hopes - all gone.

These tears I shed should melt the ice, formed by those on whom I still dream – like chance on a dice. Bathing sorrow with memories of first love's time. All my life alone – no sense, no rhyme.

Sing me a song to ease the pain, while I live through the lyrics again and again. The best of the season to you my friend, although, for the moment, the best is pretend. For the sweetness of spirits will dull out my mind.

Which way will I go? I will know as I find, the strength of the bottle help life force, decays. Think of me stumbling in a false dreamland haze.

A mention of music! More important than me. Kept me going for longer than even I would agree. Each day of composing and releasing emotion, gave me sense of achievement – an indelible potion.

No one can imagine just why thoughts change into doubts, and how sounds in the mind can let inner peace come about.

It is just a musicians Christmas without audience or even a will to play, singing sorrow and self-pity at the wine bar – like every other day.

The Visitor

"How long is Life?" she asked me just now, with curious eyes.

I turn to the mirror and see life flash by the face, of this visiting child.

Years of life's impressions and wisdom, search for an answer – yet unable to find.

With warm, kind smile and angelic face, she touches my sadness. A great weight is lifted, from my troubled mind.

Furrows of fear, eyes straining to change the mirror's cruel game, I mellow, slowly, as truth releases the realization, of an end to much pain.

"A life is as long as you care to exist. A day too soon is time lost on all those you will miss. A day too late gives anger to those who would steer your fate. A life is too short-lived – unless lived through hate."

As she fades into dream, calmness radiates, like warm fire's glow. With faint whisper,.

"Sleep long and deep. There's no more you need know."

Yet, swirling figures unscramble, performing curses in mime,

By old friends who betray me. They scream out my crimes,

Telling tales of pure anger, and foul errors in deeds,

Framed by morsels of memoirs – reaping bad crops from bad seeds.

"Oh help me, come hear me . . . for I have erred in my ways and pray to make pact – to live more useful days."

Came that face to my cheek, like a close whispering breeze, seeking more time to comfort, should such light thaw the freeze:

"With life: You can lose it – but not bring it back, stealing joy from those living for not want, but for lack . . . and desire.

There is more to just needing from people like you. Oh, I wish you had called me, before passing through."

On A Crisp English Night

Bright eyes deciphering startling glints of insight,
As misty rain falls, with some thunder and lightning seen,
Signalling time for daydreams to begin,
Inventing images of future events, on a crisp English night.
Then, remembering all the places those thoughts have been.

From high iron tower, the hungry beacon scours the land,
Over beaches, pier and holiday town – searching for answers.
Shining on children, who watch overhead wires for rainbow dancers.
Raindrops forming at random, sliding along by natures creative hand,
Simulating the pathways of life – made unique by taking chances.

These are the thoughts of home – in the heart of my mind.
Rising from foreign lands, after many years of time to reflect,
With imagination, sanity and culture, this land I now reject.
So I take to the skies in search of my kind,
To my childhood land – as best I recollect.

No More to Roam

Hear the voice within your heart,
Warning of another silent passing.
Final looks and feelings for one so small,
For whom we care – yet rarely see.

So sing a lullaby to help them to sleep,
No more to roam – so free and so wild,
In harmony with nature, heaven and Earth.
Innocently murdered, diseased or genetically scarred.

Life is for the love of simple things.

Yet, we abuse our frail surroundings too easily,

Blackening all hope for dying trees, and putrid rivers,

That wind wearily alone through salt-encrusted lands.

Spare a thought for what one can do,

To turn the tide of human waste.

The world we share, we share unjustly,

And the little children weep silently . . .

For a tiny life so brief.

The Knight's Pledge

When you rest, do you ever think of me and do you sometimes reflect on what might yet be perchance we meet again, to stare once more, misty eyed?

Nay will you find one more loving, more able to admire you for awakening my soul, in which once, silently, you seeded my willing captive role.

So on this day, I pledge my all - till death, to stare once more, and play my best hand, as I yearn each day, and scour every land, to win your heart and mind and breath.

Real People

Those who have seen her,

Say she is fighting schizophrenia,

Sleeping rough, on a damp city street.

Just an annoyance at people's feet.

No helping hand from this techno land,

While she suffers through tormented phases,

Emerging homeless, frightened and society banned,

Seen by guilty eyes with indifferent gazes.

As tapping slows from knowing cane,

Where inner friends come out and play,

From mind that copes as best for Jane,

She greets the hand, where now she lay.

"I've lost the means to see your face

Yet see your beauty in my mind.

Now sound and movement leave your trace

To your place of kindness, there to find.

Then we talk and play until the end of the day

For I made you my official guest

To share with you a wondering mind

Who sought you out to where you rest."

She smiled – he knew, for reasons told,

And he returned a waiting glance.

Then they laughed and talked until the day grew old,

Before her mind grew tired, as if it had danced.

Shadow People

Hanging about, filling in your fractured sense of time. Why do you act out life in a hazy, deranged mime?

And did you do your very best to try and fit in, when you idled along, entombed in debt, never meant to win?

But would life have been any kinder, if you could start it all again, or would pain and cold, sap your spirit dry – at the end of nameless lane?

Until, like broken, rusty vessels, you pass through life's lost parade, ending the flawed seeds of a twisted life – which your parents lovingly made. Now in a dirty, dark, crazy back-alley, craving thirsts for one last hit, as you rise above another day's pain and irreversible harm, I say to you:

Waste not one day, and change your life . . . or death will soon take all of it!

The Writer

Forever, I've travelled in search of myself,
Looking out for a life, for a person like me.
Over hills, through the skies, 'cross the wild open seas
I got lost in the void, hoping time held the key
Looking out, for a life.
Just for me!

Whenever I dream, far away in my mind
Reaching out, for a life, for a person like me.
I believe and protest, that I'll never be
Like the people who stare from the void, back at me
Reaching out, for a life
Never free!

However you know me, I'm not as I seem
Searching out, for a life
For a person like me.
I recall through blank looks and your distance from me
That you must search through life endlessly!

Well, I've seen many places and dived off life's platforms
With a mind, that was broadened, by people I've met.
Though some days I'd lose track, of all that I could be,
I never forget that dreams, make a person . . . . made me!

Song with music by Stefan Nicholson

Leaving Town

Alone in our world of destruction, I will set you free.

It is not in my heart to deny you what you want to be.

Take a look to see for yourself, that my life's gone upside down.

You don't care that I cry far too often. Now, I'm leaving town.

Through the depths of despair you have taken me, without a thought.

So I'll go alone once more, knowing you've just been caught.

I'll be free when your love turns. You're getting me down.

Just remember that we shared some good times, but now, I'm leaving town.

Song with music by Stefan Nicholson

Mother Nature

On an autumn day, when sky was blue,

She turned away, for she always knew.

Still, we clear the trees, and cull and kill.

Seeding dust to breeze, which comes in our window sill.

Trees die and then they fall

Where wild waters always flowed,

Wise tired crows would sigh and call,

Down old, abandoned red-gum road.

She turned away, and her anger grew.

We were made to pay, when the past came true.

And on that final day, when all had died,

What we tried to say, was what others hide.

Trees die and then they fall

Where wild waters always flowed,

Wise tired crows would sigh and call,

Down old, abandoned red-gum road.

The Farmer's Wife

One summer's day, back in ninety-two, she turned away from me and my stubborn point of view. Yet now I see her haunting face, with golden hair afire, in the wheat fields still a growing, as I dream in my retire.

She laughed, at my plans, of growing old and grey, with a white cane chair setting, aside my bride, with hair like hay. For all she could see, was a field of dust, all bare, just as now, from her portrait near the doorway, aside a lock of yellow hair.

I was lost for useful words, on that last day she cried, for it seemed absurd to her, to know that we'd all lied, about clearing land for the wild wind and burning sun, to bring forth full cycle, glut to lean, and all our dreams undone.

Though my face is earthy, cracked and lined, I have changed my ways to be a better man. Showing folks and kids, with an open mind, doing all I know, and should . . . and can, to love our earth, save life and pay its dues . . . then tend my resting warrior beneath green and yellow hues.

Rise Swiftly Up

Aye, you were kind of heart,

And travelled too well by bloody far.

For I've read your youth and pain, in part,

How young 'un's early rest broke hard,

Bringing mind to fray . . . then wife to part.

You were deprived of luck, yet blessed with verse,

In which I breathe your bush, and dream its sounds.

Aye, Scot of Fayal, demand I nought – nor do thee I curse,

That tragic day, when you fired that single round.

Rise swiftly up on your ghostly charger mount.

Speak thee up and take thy place – fine lad.

For you'll get full measure now, from peers that count.

New life beyond the grave – without loss like you had.

Your island homes erect to thee, fine statues tall,

And your words shine not dim, for they grow out and reach.

At last you can claim times lost, for that fateful fall,

And your wee lassie's loss . . . and for Brighton Beach.

A poem about Adam Lindsay Gordon

Night Owl's Mission

I had a dream that should I wish to choose my home, it would be where my heart lays down its burden.

Bringing restful times, to end the weary roam around foreign shores, where fiery time tamed adventurous ways, to suit the new land's cold indifferent gaze.

How thoughts grow long, when warm springtime meadows beckon, and on hearing an owl, scratching sounds from dark woody hollows, I woke up in a fright.

Just as swiftly came my aim – at least within a second, to "Reject this place where foreign wind harshly blows" each empty summer's day – towards quiet rosebush rows.

And so it came that day, as angry sun burnt more savage ochre land, turning thirsty farms to dust, and sweaty dams to lifeless sand, I sought the night, when owl glides silently over grass, and twigs and bough, like a beacon bringing wiser eyes to guide my thoughts, of getting home, somehow.

Images of crashing waves, beyond seaside life – so rich and full became silence - until caring wing drapes firm where my spirit lies. Why, it was not a crying gull, but the squadron emblem of a foreign force, that rescued England's skies.

My father has come to take me home. See how silently he flies.

Winter Golden Oaks

Branches of old golden oaks arch like the backs of stretching idle cats, embracing the damp city air, creating contrasting mercuric splendour around orange-pink hues, emanating from elegant street lamps, reflecting a warm haze through remaining stands of crumpled crusty leaves

How silent seems our natural world, as I gaze across the noisy, busy streets below. Stealthy clouds brush wistfully against squares of yellow light, adhered almost too perfectly to irregular heights of concrete cubic monoliths, illuminating the quiet city thoughts of stragglers, uncovered in fragmented sedimentary holes, where shadows creep like mist and smoke.

A gentle breeze whispers her name to arrest my blank stare, teasing final strength from each tired leaf, like fading thoughts, randomly abandoning all manner of care. Majestically gliding and spinning towards peace and finality, to return to both origin and destiny

All journeys mimic a leaf's passing, reminding and renewing moments past, where at an instant in time, life and death are at razor's edge. For that is love's magical game. A time to enjoy as an eternity, within a finite slither of nature's only plan

Why we ask ourselves the meaning of life and love is as foolish as pining for love itself. For we see its relentless change at every turn of head or sideways glance. Nature's mystery from common seed and hidden calculation is seen all around

If we spend some time when gold appears, at night's request, she will display her abandoned golden wealth as a renewable investment

The passing leaf becomes the earth, which feeds the roots and worms and seeds.

Oh, I think we are not so highly born compared to an oak tree's one acorn.

Somewhere Else

Yellow angry plumes wrestle to suckle

From a smouldering nest

Teasing the wind

As it plays along idle random paths

Within an ever-changing foreign terrain.

It is said a traitor's whim set the seed

By way of complex maniacal obsession

To bring forth forces beyond wild imagination

Abandoning with fear

Such a cruel and careless manager

Towards inevitable outcome.

Stealing vital air from human and animal squatters

The amorphous radiant beast grows stronger and more intense

Sensing freedom from human control

Over its diminishing sylvan empire.

Rising out from littered valley scrub

It erases all before it

Eating the wooded hillside bare

Consuming the putrid air before rushing blindly

To breathe new life into itself

Claiming the top of the hill

With blackened symbols of victory.

Advantageous timing allows squadrons of ember sprites

To flee immediate incineration within its breast

Amongst violent exaggerated ethereal forms

Of crimson, orange, red and powder black

To search out fresh pockets of energy

Reducing man's influence and benefit
In the cycle of natural law
To catastrophic decay and transformation
With smoke and ash
And loss and death.

The traitor has long gone, yet remains forever cursed
Tormented by guilt of wild intense moments of pleasure
Until unstable thoughts break through the sweat
Once more, from deep agonizing depression.

Now is the time that we all suffer loss
Fresh minds as ever before
Vowing never to forget lessons learned
Until time has diminished pain to memory
Like a spark which has been and gone

This war of hate from a traitor's hand
Must be matched with resolve, to fight,
To break the addictive curse
And to ready ourselves for the next time.
Next time we'll be prepared.
Next time and place ... Somewhere else.

The brave fire fighters know too well
The unpredictable cunning ways
Of the wild fire hell on earth.
For it takes no innocent hostage,
Feels no love for the wealthy, child or aged
Nor regrets ... with any emotion shown,
Consumed by its own burning desire.

We pause to make judgment on scarred survivors,

Weary volunteers and distant planners, who live with hope.

For the dead speak where they lay,

In the ashes of a maniacal play,

Though the curtain never falls for long,

Before another act begins by lighted hand

We must cry out loudly for our dead

And for the living who are damned ahead

Should we forget what matters . . .

Family,

Community,

Environment, or the hollow justice of remorse.

The Clock

"What time have you"- my conscience said,

"To find you still - wrapped up in bed?"

The clock struck four instead of eight!

Was this some new law or call of fate?

"From deep within, you could not wait,

To write all night, and rise too late."

Just then, a sharp sound pierced the room,

And the clock at once played fractured tune.

"Our dreams alone suffice as wage,

At curtain call on nature's stage."

The clock was stopped. Its springs had blown.

The pendulum lay where gears had flown.

"Your words immortal spread voice afar,"
Thought he, "Like locked within a sealed jar."
The clock stands guard o'er the writer's face.
The hands now still, they feel no pace.

My Dog

Written in Cinquain form:

My dog	(2)
Feet towards sky	(4)
Thinks not of days gone by	(6)
Warm, calm, over fed, still in bed	(8)
Faint smile	(2)

Poetry is . . .

Written in Haiku Form:

Writing poem ends	(5)
Words, pictures, colours and tone	(7)
Bringing past to life	(5)

Remembrance Day

We assemble this day to honour
And grieve for our loss
For they can no longer share
All the love and belonging
Which once they fought to protect
In the guise of our country
Draped now by its flag.

There are times like this

When loss is far too great.

For we are changed by war

Only while we remember

Each flag lying gaunt . . .

Over fragments encased.

Lost to great distance

They are missed forever,

Captured within this moment

Of quiet solitude, and regret

For time that can now never be.

Preserved by the stillness of deathly sleep,

We salute them with rifles and grand words of peace.

Yet there is no stirring from inside each flag-draped box,

On this cold and sombre day of inconsolable grief.

Melting Pot

It is the life you live within,

Not the colour of your skin

That proves the worth of who you are.

For in every quiet place, there shines a hidden star.

It is not the new language of your child,

But forgetting yours which gets you riled.

Enough to abandon thoughts of common ground,

Unless loss is outweighed by new values found.

Our past is scarred through biased rules,

Passed in great haste, thought smart by fools.

Like making changes - one right from two wrongs,

Which curse the ear from tasteless tongues.

If you give every child the gift of care,

Love for the land and sea, the people there,

It is never too early, nor ever too late

To give them much more love, than many petty ways to hate.

Time will heal — say some with doubt,

As dreaming stories sing and shout

Their meanings —for which the elders pine,

When young and wise were all of one mind.

Strayley Anne

Hayley was a wild child — bright, yet inwardly dark,

Smiling, kind and thoughtful — honesty was her mark.

Much older beyond her years she seemed

While others chose greed she observed and dreamed

About what folks wished they were, not are,

No time to cast their thoughts afar.

She saw folks willing to share all and give.

Others poor, sick and troubled - just dying to live.

Some giving in too easily with a careless wistful sigh,

Yet soldiers fight for them to live —we honour where they die.

So young Hayley tried with all her might,

To protect our world from lack of foresight.

For they lay where they fell on foreign ground in Fromelles,

"And none shall forget this," so this Australian would tell.

She forged her ground from those who fought there,

Feeling through her compassion as their souls were laid bare.

Changed her name to sound patriotically strong and proud,

To Strayley-Anne. Reborn to rise up above the crowd.

"Lest we forget," she would sigh for those she had never met,

As if listening to their orders to stand fast and to protect.

Then wondered if they would smile or frown from the darkness where they lay, or cry out loudly with angry words, to make us go away.

Katie Lane

She's a sixpenny part in a billion dollar industry.

Just another broken soul on super-highway through her misery.

Getting lonely to the point of never making day break.

Lucking out, working honestly, till she gets on the make.

Katie Lane, I'll always miss you with the chance I'll catch your gaze,

and sometimes I dream you love me and want to hold me close for days.

But you've cast your mind in sadness as you struggle to comprehend,

why your face can win a thousand loves, but broken hearts can never mend.

Take the moon in your window as my light to guide you home

And the stars as your family making sure you're not alone.

Falling rain across your window are my tears of joy and pain.

For Katie, looks and fame are fleeting, just like the falling rain.

I read your letter Kate. It said as much as I could bear.

And I wish I could have taken you to a kinder place somewhere.

But it wasn't for my eyes to see, as the news was very clear.

For they say you had a broken heart, for a love you missed so dear.

The country church stands still today, birds sing and children play.

Where once you ran so fast it hurt, to get home the quickest way.

That day I saw your awkward frame. Your laughter filled the air.

I remember when our first gaze met - the day we stopped to stare.

Now the moon in my window is a sign you are not alone.

For the stars are your family in a not too distant home.

Falling rain across my window are your tears to ease my pain.

Oh Katie, looks and fame are fleeting but our love will never wane.

Song with music by Stefan Nicholson

Another Night on my Street

I watched you last night, as you screamed like a spoilt child.

Swearing loudly, enraged from your careless ideals.

Smashing bottles, causing mayhem, just a nuisance, bred defiled.

Your body, frail and limp with drugs, degrading as it heals.

Oh, you looked so hopeless and weak, as you fell down to your knees

Like your parents - lying drunk in your dysfunctional home.

It is true that the nut does not fall far from the trees,

Regardless of wealth or where you schooled or the distance that you roam.

Cheeky Monkey

You will never ever catch me

As I jump and swing around

On your table, 'cross the lounge room,

Through the air – then gone to ground.

I am yellow like a 'nana,

With a wit to test your nerves

But you'll never ever catch me

With my twists and turns and swerves.

I will tease you, never leave you

And if you try to pin me down,

Then I will play up like I am at the zoo

To make you squirm and frown.

Moonlight Grey

Some winners give and take high-fives

But my Zoe flips to live nine lives.

Always fooling, chasing dreams, making a play.

Just highway roaming for each chance to waylay.

'Cos she's a rolling blur of moonlight grey

With a nose white-tipped every night and all day

I'm saying, that you always know when she "arrives"

'Cos my Zoe flips to live nine lives

Cass soon turned that Zoe upside of down,

Had her looking like a corpse with a worn-out frown.

Sharing space, friends, and sometimes love.

'Till poor Cass went "one-way". Cos she was called up from above.

Yeah, she's a rolling blur of moonlight grey

With a nose white-tipped every night and all day

I'm saying, that you always know when she "arrives"

'Cos my Zoe flips to live nine lives

She calls morning and night, screaming out her demands.

Hey, just don't pull her strings with a hesitant hand,

She's no puppet. Cos like when she strikes, you will bleed,

All steamed for revenge, when you don't fix her needs.

Oh yeah. She's a rolling blur of moonlight grey,

With a nose white-tipped every night and all day.

I'm saying, that you always know when she "arrives",

'Cos my Zoe flips to live nine lives.

The Majesty of Life

Nature's jewel shines not only upon the finger ring but within each glance, where we see everything that sways the senses, calms the breath and feeds the inner soul from birth to death with riches far beyond the tools of man - displayed within the beauty of a delicate plan.

Imagine a whale's journey or the migration of wild herds, for the majesty of life cannot be explained in simple words.

Just compare Earth's night sky with moon and sprinkled stars, to the mountains and rivers, oceans deep and tree-lined bays with bars. And see that a common hand has touched each one with fresh palette, to follow once each season has almost gone. It seems there is a cyclic spell, yet with random chance of change to make sea and lake become cloud and rain - sand and fire to mountain range.

Lands of greens and browns with sky and sea of different blues perceived by using light and dark, combining waves of special hues. And for each breath we take from the very time we're born, we feel the trees return a breath refreshed, starting every early morn.

Rainy days, summer afternoons, winter nights and stormy seas, misty rain breathing on faces like a cool light-hearted tease.

Resonance feeding between the physical and imagined thoughts which we keenly perceive and cherish and keep safe within our forts..

All this splendour is a wonder from some far, far distant throne, which we accept lightly far too often with blind familiarity, as if we're all alone.

There is strength in idle thoughts like a daydream coming true, making sense of an unknowing, providing firm belief on cue.

Visualising both origin and destiny as like the random path of man exposing seeds of calculation as part of this grand majestic plan.

So rejoice each child who falters, yet gets up each time they fall, then spends a lifetime learning secrets, to why there is majesty at all.

Back to Hobart

If you're heading back to Hobart on an autumn day,

You will see the mountain rising over Sandy Bay.

When you feel that light wind blowing up from old Iron Pot,

Then, you know you're surely blessed with what you've got.

Come and roam our island home

You will always have a place to call your own.

Hear the wind call you home

It's time. Return with sails aloft, full blown.

Have you heard the cat play fiddle in the city mall

Or have you shopped in Salamanca at a market stall

Or explored the Channel sailing out from Oyster Cove?

Oh, there is always somewhere close to rest or rove.

Come and roam, fresh air and crashing foam,

See the rolling hills and rivers flow.

Hear the wind call you home.

It is time. Return with sails aloft, full blown.

Song with music by Stefan Nicholson

Buzzzzz

I know I've never Thylacine
Unless it happened when I have jumping been.
Shhhh! Have I just now, a lion snoring heard?
Or could it maybe be a bee trapped in my lemon curd?

Buzzzzzzzzzzzz   Buzzzzzzzzzzzzz

Where is that river, now just where did Derwent?
Did it fall from mountain top, in a watery descent?
Amongst the clouds, with wind and rain so clear.
Whoa, look! I can see all around Tasmania.

First Call

A child reaches out from poverty and constant daily fears. Her innocent mind withdrawn in sadness aside her parent's tears, with little chance of getting help from someone, sometime, somewhere, betrayed by those who should educate, protect and love with care.

Yet each tear awakens a call to action to change her impoverished land, as awareness, feelings and compassion reach out to lend a hand.

To make a start is to understand and reason how hard it is to try to change her life and comprehend why some choose to let her die.

Why do they live and die this way, while others look away? Well I will show you greed and apathy, and what we waste . . . and why children can't safely play. And why, underneath the starry sky the homeless try to sleep, abandoned but for nuisance sake at their fellow human's feet.

We fight for just equality, freedom from domination. Yet we sacrifice ordinary quiet lives and soldiers from each nation. Then for a while, just a finite time, each life is loved and saved, until new wealth and power are unjustly gained. The poor once more enslaved.

With open heart and strength of mind we move in to take a stand. First to understand each problem close, in some unfamiliar land. Then we teach the folks to help themselves to feed and work and live, for this is the gift that lasts forever . . . for first they take, before they give.

Silly Thoughts

Sitting on my patch of earth

I thought much about what my life is worth.

Thinking much about my dear child's birth,

Wondering how it will grow, what it will be,

When I am gone,

When he is me.

Spinning round and round the plasma sun

Sounds silly really and not much fun.

From there the greens look changed to brown,

And food is short,

And days are long.

We never really stood a chance.

Yet I sit here now resolute but slightly more askance.

Stay Awhile

Stay awhile and I'll befriend you, calm your mind to feel at home, put my arm around your shoulder, so near danger you'll not roam and gently ask you reconsider why you think it is time to go, as I share with you compassion, though the wind will gust and blow.

Don't say a word. That stage has passed. For we sit along this concrete ledge, with cold and rain and accomplice wind, that all but seem to pledge to steer you from harm and bring you down for being in such a wretched place, as many would soon be deeply hurt, if no more they will see your face.

But wait, you only need more time for thought about the position in which your choice is caught, between leaving, staying, working things out, for together we can break this curse, to see fact and reason as they really are.

So come with me and trust my word, knowing you will now be safe, no matter how absurd it seems to you. For I once heard those words like you . . . before a kindly friend did help me too.

The Gale

Blow as hard as you will to hasten dark clouds

With such pace as to obscure sun's warmth and light,

To irritate each seldom restful mind.

Now they all despise your reckless spirit.

For you bring undone all manner of human existence

As you sweep away our toil without so much as a care,

With a festering hate for whatever meets to resist you,

Extinguishing any love once held for your might,

As we suffer your psychotic frenzied temper.

And much like love, we have no say over your intended duration,

For you conceal your form which can never be tamed,

By making each beginning and end reside beyond our grasp.

So blow as hard as you will to hasten your passing,

For you will soon be spent . . . and forgotten.

Dandelion

Dandelion you have sent out your envoy seeds

Perchance to roam and swirl on the wind of destiny.

Beyond which sits a dragonfly, quietly alert,

Askew, askance, smiling inwardly

On my ponderous idle thinking.

We do so aimlessly in elaborate reflection
Exhausting our flair for idle folly
Seemingly born within each human mind,
Preoccupied by that pious lingering pretence.
Proclaiming we alone are elect to be free
From nature's complex intricate bind.

My surface pretends agreement for society . . . but I am not thee!
Fending those who hope to change my ways, my voice, my eyes that see.
Yet will I relent to power or wealth, or trade my values for a fee?
No . . . Not even when the last I breathe,
For no-one speaks or acts for me.

Don't Follow Anyone

Don't worry about your looks, or seek shallow fame or wealth.
Look at the stars to inspire different thoughts within yourself.
Stand up for your beliefs and fight for what you know is right.
See the real you, not the fake in what they say in all their hype.
Learn to rise above life's failures and fly freely like a kite.
Don't follow anyone going nowhere, just to be in vogue.
You are a star. You are a hero, with a little bit of rogue.
You are young enough to change the world in many different ways.
You are a soldier of your future. You are meant for peaceful days.

Moment in Time

If you have the time and energy to write, then write but if you should find yourself dreaming, then dream as if you are participating in your story.

Living and dreaming are both real to the writer's mind, yet they reside in different dimensions of time.

We live only in the present, for the past has gone.

The future is only a possibility based on how we live within each moment and how we interact with random events that cross our chosen paths.

My Astral Girl

I dreamt about an astral girl whose life I shared in a cosmic swirl.

And just for a while I spun around and around, entwined in her dreams, entangled in her cloud.

On stars we floated closely by, 'cross the forests, sea and heavenly sky. I was captured by her purest love, yet she climbed higher, far above, over valleys, hills and misty streams – and all that was, in the in-betweens.

Still she soared much higher, away from me, for I'd dreamt far too much, too far to see, not heeding what the wise moon had said, as I lay dreaming on my bed . . . her image frozen in my head.

"Please only see her as a friend,

So your astral dream may never end."

I still dream about an astral girl whose life I shared in a cosmic swirl and it makes my mind spin around and around and around, entwined in her dreams, entangled in her cloud.

Then I thank the moon for being so kind, when it shines through my window, to comfort my mind.

Kate and Me

I staggered half-dressed into the wild saloon to say sorry I was late.

She was fully dressed, unlike her old mate and said, "You know you came too soon?"

So I answered slyly, "Don't think that, my wondrous Kate, for we were only meant to spoon."

Well, if the piano had creaked and squeaked all night – it was clearly out of tune, as Kate and me just held on tight until I squeezed her up and doon.

Then wasn't that a funny sight – silhouetted against the moon.

Malcolm Magpie (the poem)

A magpie sat on my TV, and started singing instantly.

I said, "What are you doing, singing like that, 'cos I've fed you lean, so you won't get fat!"

But Malcolm Magpie – that's his name, said my excuse was rather lame. Then he pointed to the advert with a huge meat pie, and squawked, "Get me one of those and away I'll fly."

Well. I got a huge meat pie from the baker, and the doctor gave me a second-hand pacemaker – just in case Malcolm's arteries could not cope. Aye he thinks his smart but he is really such a dope.

When he saw the meat pie, he gulped it down and true to his word, flew off to town. But he was really searching out for that baker's shop, even though he could feel he was about to pop!

So, he strapped up the pacemaker to his fat, wobbly chest. No silly Malcolm – it goes under your vest!

And when he dropped from the sky, from the pressure of that huge meat pie, people thought he would explode . . . and they quickly passed him by!

That is everyone except one. Yes . . . of course it was me!

For the outcome was expected, I knew what it would be and why I followed greedy Malcolm Magpie, with a strong cup of tea.

Note: This was made into a children's short story

My Friend

My friend has a pet that he won as a bet.

Sort of roundly square, with tufts of rough blue hair.

It has no bottom. It has no top.

All I can see is a middle

And that I believe is the lot.

He calls it "Spit" but it does not know its name

Which is just as well I am told in haste,

'cos it looks from both ends, just the same!

It keeps one eye on its food in the big red shiny bowl.

But I always put it back on its face in the hole.

The other eye just stares at the stars in night's sky.

I swear that this is true, but I am more prone to lie.

It is true that my friend has a pet.

Part bird, part giraffe and flies a private jet.

You must all believe that I could not possibly conceive

In my wildest dreams, such a creature . . . .

That is calm and cute and soft but sometimes . . .

may also . . . **eat you!**

Roxy Dog

Livie phoned me up and said today that she didn't want to go out – or to play. Well I tried to understand - when she said, "Dreams only come true, if you stay in bed."

Then she drew a "C" on a rock, see. Believing that the rock would unlock, see.

Rock - C - Rock - C

Roxy! Roxy Dog!

So I went to see her older sister, to tell her to get up , we really missed her. She said, "I dreamt about a dog that needs release."

And then made a "C" with her hand, did our Elisse.

Yes she drew a "C" on a rock, see. Believing that the rock would unlock, see.

Rock - C - Rock - C

Roxy! Roxy Dog!

Now the next time when I saw them, there were three, see. Livie and Elisse and a dog, see. I said, "Is that the dog you dreamed in bed, that must now be walked each day and fed?" Then they both pointed where their dream rock used to be.

Yes they once drew a "C" on a rock see

Believing that the rock would unlock, see.

Rock - C - Rock - C

Roxy! Roxy Dog!

This is now a children's song

Her Style

I still dream that I see her . . . that lady I loved,

For she shines like the moon, fairest maiden above,

With such air and deportment, that gives her away.

An image in my thoughts throughout the rest of each day

She is a portrait of spring embodied in youth,

Far away in my mind, but closer than the truth.

Yet when I did catch a quick glance, which swept me faint with her style, distracted she passed by me . . . for a more fervent smile.

Windswept

Windswept, dark-grey, cold sombre moods.

Towel-draped.

So sad and blue.

Silent movements.

Deep-sighing.

Cute!

Remembering now, life's simple rule:

"When summer ends . . . it's time for school".

48

Xavier's Wheels

Zoe told me the story about a hero boy

Who laughs out loud as he crashes each toy

And his name is Xavier.

A little rascal having fun – it was not bad behaviour.

Now when a giant stole all the wheels

(To eat with his glass and plastic meals

And two fat horses and a yellow duck)

Taken from cars and planes and a monster truck,

Then the world we knew was not the same.

Until Xavier hatched a plan – now this was no game!

Zoe said her brother worked hard for days on end

To make a pie that he could send

To the giant's house high up in the sky.

It was a round-wheel pastry potato pie.

Xavier pushed the pie through the giant's letterbox.

Then off to the front door, where he knock, knock, knocks!

The giant shouted angrily "Who is there?"

For to have a visitor, why it was so extremely rare.

"I've baked a giant pie in the shape of a wheel,

And I've come to offer it to you as a special deal.

For our cars and planes and trucks stand still.

And if you eat all our wheels, it will surely make you ill.

So if you give them back, why I promise you

That I will bake another pie – maybe one, maybe two.

But you must promise now that no more will you steal.

Especially each driving, steering, meant-for- moving wheel."

Do You Want To Know?

Do you want to know the words of every love song that you've heard? Well there's a time I do, but not when I'm alone.

For love really hurts when it ends and every word spoken makes you realise it's gone. Some know it's the time when you just can't carry on.

For you're gone away from me, and I'll no longer be that most treasured part, of your warm and loving heart, and I'll never believe that your love's not meant for me.

But with thoughts of your loving misty eyes, now making someone else to sigh, it makes no more sense to me. For what once was bound has now set me free.

Do you want to know my thoughts that all our precious moments taught? Where I tried to understand then later call you?

But then your last look made it clear, that you just don't want me near to your heart . . . to your heart. You don't want me near to your heart.

For you're gone away from me, and I'll no longer be that most treasured part, of your warm and loving heart, and I'll never believe that your love's not meant for me.

Yet thoughts of your loving misty eyes, now making someone else to sigh. Well, it makes no more sense to me, that what once was happy bound has now set me sadly free.

Song with music by Stefan Nicholson

For I Told Myself You Loved Me

If you ever hear this song my love

Know it was written just for you.

I wrote it staring at the stars above

When we were one . . . not two.

I hear the falling rain as the beating of your heart

And you are just a mime, no longer tearing me apart.

Cos when I looked into the mirror's eyes

I saw the truth . . . our love was lies.

Yet I told myself so often . . . that you loved me.

Like a rush of air you consumed my soul and mind,

Like a firestorm brewing, the passion rising up to find

An opportunity in which to devour me whole.

Yet I stand before you, strong . . . upright and tall,

In defiance to your game to make me fall,

To make me sad. To build your wall.

Now I look anew through the mirror's eyes

To make sure my spirit always flies.

Cos you once said, like from a book you may have read

That I may be that special one . . . if only you could love me.

Song with music by Stefan Nicholson

Just Want to Say

Just want to say that I'm sad you needed time to go away.

It was such an unexpected feeling, for you had told me softly only yesterday.

Was it something that I did? Or maybe feelings that you hid?

Tell me what I need to do. Show me how we're ever going to get us through. You and me just need a clue, in this world of our own making.

You stole my heart and I just can't take more pain. Must we grow apart with each of us to blame?

Cos you once said, you would be very hard to tame, but I did not know that you were only playing a game.

Song with music by Stefan Nicholson

Like a Mermaid

I catch your glance as I pass by, yet never know if I can reach you.

Where, true love asks not why, dream-like thoughts sweep by.

Do you feel it too? I wonder.

Hear me . . . me.

Can you understand my ways?

For the difference is . . . why, it's only, slight – least I think so.

But who am I?

Can I live in your world?

Wait! If I should leave here, I can never, ever go back to my home.

Forever would I roam. I'd always be alone.

Without you.

I catch your glance as I pass by, yet never know if I can reach you.

Where, true love asks not why, Dream-like thoughts sweep by,

Do you feel it too?

I wonder. . .

Do you feel it too?

Song with music by Stefan Nicholson

About the author:

Stefan Nicholson, MA (Swinburne) has had a multiple career in science and technology with an unstoppable undercurrent to author books and compose music.

He is the author of fourteen books which include novels, short stories, poetry and an invented international symbol language called "Symbolic Art Notation".

Stefan has also composed more than fifty musical compositions producing a DVD "Pictures of Life" with twenty of them recorded on seventeen tracks for full orchestra and band.

He is a member of the Australian Society of Authors, a Fellow of the Institute of Scientific and Technical Communicators and has spent fifteen years as a Technical Writer and Multi-Media designer.

Born in England with a Polish father before migrating to Tasmania, Stefan now lives in Hobart, Tasmania on his boat "Nickinoff" in the Prince of Wales Bay Marina.

www.ingramcontent.com/pod-product-compliance
Lightning Source LLC
Chambersburg PA
CBHW020320150626
46552CB00022B/3041